The Ten Plagues of Egypt

The Ten Plagues

by Shoshana Lepon

Illustrated by Aaron Friedman

The Judaica Press • 1998 • New York

# of Egypt

„ולמען תספר באזני בנך ובן–בנך את אשר התעללתי במצרים...'' (שמות י:ב)

''And you shall tell in the ears of your sons and your son's son how I made fun of Egypt...'' (Exodus 10:2)

To the children of the
Diaspora Yeshiva Day School
Mt. Zion, Israel

A special thanks

To my parents, Dr. and Mrs. David Loev

To Rabbi Mordechai Goldstein, *shlita,* Rosh Yeshiva of Diaspora Yeshiva,

whose love of Torah and belief in *chazal* are an example to all his students

To Michael Strum whose creative sketches formed the basis

of many of the drawings for this book

To my friend and consultant Yeshara Gold

And to my husband for his constant support

© Copyright 1988
THE JUDAICA PRESS, INC.
New York, N.Y.

First Impression, 1988
Second Impression, 1994
Third Impression, 1998

Library of Congress Catalog Card No. 87-83636

ISBN: 0-910818-77-0 Hardbound Edition
ISBN: 0-910818-76-2 Softbound Edition

Printed in Singapore

Come hear the great tale
Of a rich mighty land
Whose wicked king wanted
To fight G-d's command.

Egypt's king, Pharaoh,
Had Israel enslaved,
But G-d had decided
That they should be saved.

5

G-d wanted His people
To live by His plan;
To follow His law
For the good of each man.

So Moses was sent
To tell Pharaoh G-d's word:
"Send out My people!
Their cry has been heard!"

6

But the king saw no reason
To set his slaves free.
He boasted: "No ruler
Is greater than me!"

"Who is G-d?!" Pharaoh laughed,
"That He orders me so?
I rule the Israelites.
They shall not go!"

7

This foolish king's future
Would soon be undone...
Of the Ten Plagues of Egypt
Blood was plague number one.

Blood oozed from the rivers
Like thick, sticky jelly.
Dead fish made the waters
Disgusting and smelly.

Blood in the bathtub,
And blood in the sink;
No water at all—
Not a drop left to drink.

The only fresh water
Was found by the slaves.
"Let us drink," begged their masters,
"Or we'll go to our graves."

But the moment the Israelites
Shared a few sips,
The water turned bloody
On the Egyptians' lips.

Even Pharaoh was thirsty,
But still he said, "No!
They want to serve G-d?
Well, I won't let them go!"

9

Said Moses to Pharaoh,
"Why don't you give in?
You're fighting with G-d!
Don't you know you can't win?"

Next came the second plague:
Frogs, big and bumpy.
They hid in the houses
And made people jumpy.

They sprang from the rivers,
Dripping and slimy,
Rolling in bedsheets
And making them grimy.

In the kitchens of Egypt
The ovens were shaking,
With frogs leaping out of
The bread that was baking.

10

Frogs hopped onto shoulders
And croaked into ears.
They made such a racket,
It brought one to tears.

But the frogs only made
Pharaoh's stubbornness grow:
"These are my slaves!
I shall not let them go!"

11

Said Moses, "Two plagues,
And you still don't agree?
Perhaps you'll give in
After plague number three.

"Being cruel to the Israelites
Carries a price.
All Egypt's dust
Will now turn to lice!"

12

They came for a visit,
Those unwanted guests,
And no magic helped
To get rid of the pests.

Egyptians tried soaking
In rivers and springs,
But still could not flee
From the small, itchy things.

Others took cover
In tunnels down deep
But way underground
Lice continued to creep.

Shouted Pharaoh, "I'm ruler
Above and below!
Nothing can force me
To let my slaves go!"

But Moses just said,
"Oh, you arrogant king.
You've suffered three plagues
Without learning a thing."

Then Egypt shook
With a deafening roar...
Wild beasts stalked the streets
In plague number four.

Breaking down doors
And charging up stairs
Were lions and leopards
And mean grizzly bears.

Egyptians hid, trembling,
In barrels and boxes,
Protecting themselves
From mad dogs and foxes.

Pharaoh hurried to Moses:
"I'll free them today!
Just please have your G-d
Drive these creatures away!"

But when the beasts left,
Evil Pharaoh said, "No!"
And took back his promise:
"I won't let them go."

15

Said Moses, "Beware!
G-d is fighting our battle
Because you have treated us
Worse than your cattle.

"Israelites struggle
With wagons and plows
While you give rest
To your oxen and cows.

"But the cows that you pamper
To grow fat and thick—
With plague number five
Will be terribly sick."

So ill were those cows
They could not even moo;
They lay around helpless,
With no strength to chew.

But the Israelites' cows
Had no coughs and no wheezes,
No chills and no fevers,
No sniffles or sneezes.

Cried Pharaoh, "I'm king here!
And my slaves must know
If they want to serve G-d—
I shall not let them go!"

17

But the greatest of kings
Have no strength on their own.
The power to rule
Is in G-d's hands alone.

Stubborn king Pharaoh
Was acting absurd.
How foolish to think
He would have the last word!

G-d sent plague number six—
Hot, watery blisters—
On aunts and on uncles,
On brothers and sisters.

On man and on beast
Those boils kept doubling;
All over their bodies
Big blotches were bubbling.

It swelled up on bellies,
This dreaded disease.
It burst out on elbows,
On knuckles and knees.

Even Pharaoh had boils
From forehead to toe,
But he wouldn't bend:
"My slaves shall not go!"

Then Egypt was warned
About plague number seven:
Hailstones like boulders
Would rain down from heaven.

Most people did not need
To hear any more.
They ran into their houses
And bolted each door.

But the ones who were headstrong
Ignored all advice;
They stayed in their fields
And were struck down by ice.

Hail fell down, flaming,
With flashes of lightning
And loud bursts of thunder
That made it more frightening.

20

Pharaoh quickly called Moses:
"They're free men, I swear!"
And just then the hail stopped—
It stopped in mid-air.

But then Pharaoh laughed:
"For a few flakes of snow
Did you really expect me
To let my slaves go?"

21

Said Moses, "The eighth plague
Will be armies of locusts!"
Cried the king, "I'm not frightened
By your hocus-pocus."

Pharaoh's men begged,
"Save what's left of our land!"
But still he refused
To heed G-d's command.

The locusts invaded
And made their attack,
Munching grapes from the vines
22   For a mid-morning snack.

And when they got down
To some serious eating,
Every tree in the land
Took a terrible beating.

Pharaoh called Moses;
He wasted no time:
"I've enslaved them too long!
I admit to my crime!"

But when the plague stopped
Wicked Pharaoh said, "No!"
He again changed his mind:
"My slaves shall not go!"

23

The ninth plague gave Egypt
A horrible fright:
Three days of thick darkness;
Not one ray of light.

For being so wicked,
So heartless and mean,
This dark was the darkest
To ever be seen.

Whoever tried walking
Could not lift his feet,
And anyone sitting
Was stuck to his seat.

But the slaves were now blessed
With miraculous light;
It shone in the daytime
And even at night.

Pharaoh said, "Moses,
I'll free them today!
The people may go,
But the animals stay."

"But our flocks," said Moses,
"Are needed, you know."
"Sorry," said Pharaoh,
"I won't let them go!"

25

"The tenth plague," said Moses,
"Is surely the worst...
You've time yet to stop it;
I'm warning you first..."

But foolhardy Pharaoh
Felt somehow he'd win.
His land all but ruined—
Still he wouldn't give in...

26

In the quiet of night
Loud cries filled the air...
Egyptians were weeping
And pulling their hair...

In the houses of Egypt
The oldest sons died—
For no one had listened
When G-d's children cried.

"Leave my land!" ordered Pharaoh
"I surrender to you!
Take your people, your cattle,
And pray for me, too!"

Egyptians were pressing them
Not to be slow:
"You've made enough trouble!
Get moving, now! Go!"

The slaves rushed, not waiting
For their dough to rise,
But the future would bring them
A dreadful surprise...

For Pharaoh, of course,
Changed his mind once again,
Chasing after the Israelites
With Egypt's armed men...

28

The sea split for Israel
To cross on dry ground...
Then it came crashing back,
And the soldiers were drowned.

Great Egypt lay ruined,
With many men dead,
And the slaves were now free
With their homeland ahead.

No more need the Israelites
Fear any man.
With G-d as their master,
True freedom began.

Attacked from all sides
They marched into the sea...
But faith in G-d's mercy
Would soon make them free.

29

Questions for Review and Discussion

1 What happened when the Egyptians tried to drink the Israelite's water in plague no. 1?

2 What was so unpleasant about the plague of frogs?

3 What did the Egyptians do to the Israelites that they deserved to lose their cattle in plague no. 5?

4 What did the Egyptians do to try to escape from the lice? Did it help?

5 Did the boils affect people only?

6 What happened to the hail when Pharaoh agreed to free his slaves? Did he keep his word?

7 How long did the plague of darkness last?

8 Pharaoh was more stubborn than the rest of the Egyptians. Find proof in the story.

9 Why did the Egyptians push the slaves to go after plague no. 10?

10 What do we eat every year to remind us of how quickly the Israelites left Egypt?

11 Did the Israelites wait for the sea to split before they marched across? Did they know beforehand that it would split? What does this teach us about the Israelites?

12 How do the Ten Plagues of Egypt teach that G-d created the world?

Did You Know That...

♣ During plague no. 1 the Israelites had clean water, but when the Egyptians touched it, it turned to blood. The only way the water would stay clean for the Egyptians was when it was bought for gold and silver. The Israelites grew wealthy during the plague of blood by selling water to the Egyptians, and were thus repaid for some of the hard work they had done over their years of slavery. *(Exodus Rabbah* 89)

♣ The plague of frogs actually began with one giant frog that rose out of the Nile. The Egyptians beat this frog with sticks, and everytime they beat it, it split up into many smaller frogs, until the entire land was filled with little frogs.

   The plague of frogs settled a fight between Egypt and Ethiopia. For years, they had argued about where the border was between the countries and who owned the land. Then the frogs came and covered the land of Egypt, but they would not step one foot outside Egypt's border. And so everyone saw where the border was! *(Exodus Rabbah)*

♣ Plague no. 7 brought a miracle within a miracle. Not only did this strange hail fall only on Egyptian homes and fields, it was made of fire and ice, two opposites working together!

♣ In order to show that the Israelites were not being punished by the plague of darkness, G-d gave them light even during the night.

♣ The sea did not split for the Israelites until they jumped into the water.

   When the Red Sea split, all the water, in every land, all over the world, split as well. In oceans, rivers, lakes, puddles, tubs, bowls and cups, the water split down the middle and people all over the earth knew that a miracle was happening and the Israelites were being freed.

♣ Some sources say that Pharaoh survived the Red Sea and set up a new kingdom in Nineveh. He was the ruler in the days of Jonah. Pharaoh seemed to have finally learned his lesson, for he quickly repented when Jonah warned him of G-d's displeasure.

About the Author

Shoshana Lepon teaches advanced Judaic studies at the Diaspora Yeshiva Women's Seminary in the Old City of Jerusalem. She lives on Mount Zion, adjacent to the ancient site of King David's Tomb, with her husband, a teacher of Talmud, and their four children. Mrs. Lepon has written a series of children's books on biblical subjects, including *The Ten Tests of Abraham,* published by the Judaica Press, Inc., in 1986.